Cover by Craig Holland Art.

Designed and published in the USA, 2021.

All the names, stories, places, likenesses, etc. are fictional.

Any likeness or similarity is purely coincidental.

Dedicated to Mom. Never a fall adventure was more fun than in a pumpkin patch with the one who loved it more than I do. She told me to always have an imagination for Fall.

Chapter 1

It was a cool fall day in the middle of October, in the year that is not quite the present, but not the past. The wind likes this time of year to blow leaves around and around until they are so dizzy, they don't remember what is up and what is down, what is right and what is left. Children love this so they can find a large pile of said leaves, ripe for leaping into. The leaves spew in all sorts of directions.

Flowing this way and that, the patterns they create are ones that can never be drawn on paper. Well, except maybe those who are not paying attention when using a pen. Another warm feeling people have during October is that of pumpkin pie. Now, some can eat the pie warm, some eat it cold. But the delicious orange colored vegetable is actually fruit!

This can be as shocking to a child as when they find out that Santa Claus actually does fly around the world in one night. If you don't believe me, then you can write a letter yourself, and ask. The address is Santa Claus Lane, North Pole, Alaska, 99705. Mr. Claus couldn't live on top of the North Pole. That would be impractical. Think of all the trouble he would have making all those gifts on unsettled ice.

Instead, he chose a quiet portion of what we know as Alaska. I don't know what others would call it.

This revelation often comes harder when it comes from a mother. There is no thing held against fathers. Yet, when a mother has to tell her child that a pumpkin isn't quite what it seems, or that the pie is actually made from something else, it can be quite a shock. This stems from mother nature. Telling something you bore and raised that they potentially have been misled regarding their favorite fall food is nearly heartbreaking.

This is the exact sort of thing to happen to Neil and his Mother.

"Mother, where do pumpkins come from?" That was the start of the unfortunate conversation.

She was busy rolling the dough for the pie crust to set in the circle shaped tin, "Well, they come from a pumpkin patch."

"What is a pumpkin patch? Is it a place in a market?"

Mother laughed. "No, you silly boy, it is a farm for pumpkins. They usually have a corn maze too."

"They sell pumpkins?" he asked.

"Oh yes," she replied.

"And the corn too?" he asked.

"Some do," she replied.

"Are they large pumpkins?" he asked.

"Some are really large. They take those to local fairs, and farmers markets," she replied.

"Why?" he asked.

"So they can show their hard work off. And win money."

"So they can buy more pumpkins to plant?" he asked.

"More seeds, yes," she replied.

"Seeds?" he asked.

"Why, yes, where do you think pumpkins come from?" she replied.

"Where do they buy the seeds?" he asked.

It was at this stage in the talking, that Mother wanted to focus on more the pie. "I don't know. I suppose someone has them somewhere."

"Do we need more pumpkins?"

His mother looked at the one in front of her. It was enough to make one pie, but not to carve in a jack-o'-lantern.

"How about you go get me some more pumpkin seeds for us to plant? And see if you can find suitable pumpkins to carve. Mr. Dodson has a good patch. Just down the way."

Mr. Dodson was one of those neighbors who apparently did not mind having children stop by unannounced to nab the pumpkins from him for the use of carving them. Neil thought this made him very kind and trustworthy.

Without another word of conversation, he set off down the road. Now, mind you this is an old-fashioned country road. Complete with dusty old-dirt, and that smell of dirt mixed with old mud from the morning dew.

It was these roads that Mothers did not worry when their children were sent out to get pumpkins from their neighbors for pies, for most people passing through were friendly enough, if there were any passing through at all.

This was especially true on this fine day. The sun was out and the crows were able to watch any passerby with a watchful gaze. At the first sign of trouble they would crow and crow and crow, warning them to listen. Mother always told Neil to watch carefully at the crows. If they flew, he should fly. If they stood still, he should stand still. When asked why, she told him this:

"Now, the crows are good watchers. They fly in groups, meaning more eyes to warn you of danger. Mama Crows are protective of all children. Whether their own, or not."

Neil was curious about if other creatures were as friendly.

"Oh yes. Cats and dogs. People think they are very different. But they always watch over any young ones. No matter what they are."

This made it easier for Neil to not be afraid when he ventured on his own through the fields or the woods just beyond. Having so many mothers out there looking out for him, he wondered why.

"Because no matter where they come from, all Mamas know what it is like to have a young one of their own. It's a sense that is a part of all our hearts. Sharing it with children."

So off Neil went on his way to Mr. Dodson's farm, knowing he was safe.

Chapter 2

The sun was warm as always, but there was no wind. This made Neil a little warmer than he would like during his long and arduous journey.

He needed shade to cool off. And perhaps some lemonade. Or tea. People usually had that sort of thing. There would be someone to help travelers or those in need Mother always said.

First thing was first, he needed to find a big ol' tree to sit under. He paused on the dirt road. He had been walking for some time and his feet were tiring from carrying him so far.

He spotted a large oak tree just off the side of the road. The shade would be perfect for him to rest. With a quick nap in mind, he sat down and leaned against the bark.

It would do no harm to close his eyes would it?

No. He thought it would not. His mother asked him to go to Mr. Dodson's but did not say how long it should take him. Besides, such a nice day would be wasted if not enjoyed.

With a small yawn, he fell asleep under the tree's shade.

After a time, he felt a pain in his left leg. It was not his dream. That was about him sailing down a river.

Rubbing his eyes open, he saw a large crow on his leg, pecking at it.

"Crow! What are you doing? Shoo. Shoo."

The bird stopped what it was doing and seemed to look at him. With its head tilted to the side, it hopped over his kneecap to get a better look at him.

"Please do not 'shoo' me," the Crow said. She sounded annoyed.

Neil rubbed his eyes further. Then picked his ears. "I'm sorry. I…I didn't know."

"You 'shoo' me, I could 'shoo' you for sitting under a tree in the middle of the road. Do you know how dangerous that is?" She flapped her wings at her side for emphasis.

Neil look down the road to his left. Then to his right. He saw no danger. "But there isn't anyone around."

"I'm around. How do you know that I am not dangerous? And don't start a sentence with the word 'but'. It's improper grammar."

"Sorry. What should I use?"

"'However' would do fine. Or better yet, the word 'yet'."

He thought for a moment. The bird knew what she was talking about since she sounded so confident.

"You seem fine and not dangerous in the slightest bit. Although you were poking me just then."

"I could be mean! I could rob you! You couldn't the slightest any idea if I were dangerous or not."

"Are you?"

She huffed her feathers. "No. I am trying to help you."

Neil smiled. "I didn't know birds could talk."

"They can't. Crows can. And owls. They are so pretentious though. Others can, although I have not met many of them personally."

"Why are they pretentious?"

"They flaunt their wisdom. Although, I haven't met one that had more wisdom than I."

"Doesn't that make you pretentious too?"

She laughed and cawed, "So it does! What a small world. Now young one, where are you headed? I shall guide you there safely."

"I am going to Mr. Dodson's to get pumpkins for my mother."

"Then Mr. Dodson's it is! Let us be off!"

With that the Crow hopped off his legs and scrambled a few feet in front of him, opening and closing her wings.

It seemed to Neil that she was excited for this adventure. Perhaps it would be exciting!

Chapter 3

Neil got to his feet and brushed off his pants. Mother always told him to try and be neat at all times.

"Now, appearance is good when meeting with people. Especially at the start."

"Why?"

"It shows that you care about yourself and others."

Ever since, Neil made sure that he tried his hardest to be nice and neat.

With that they started off down the road. What a pair they made. A boy and his newfound friend. She started to flutter and then flew in circles above him.

"Neil!" She called down to him. She flew down in front of him.

"Cows!"

"Cows?" he asked.

"Cows! There are cows blocking the road. A man is trying to herd them back in."

He put his hand to his brow and squinted his eyes. Indeed, cows were just ahead. A man in a yellow wicker hat was trying to push one back into the field.

When he and the Crow approached, a big brown cow stared at him from the road. The man was leaning his shoulder against it, trying to push them across to an opening in the fence, which had some wire strewn about.

"Hello Cow," Neil said, he rubbed the nose of the cow and its lips tugged at his shirt then was prompted to moo.

"MOOOOOOO."

The man laughed, "Hello there! I see you met Celia."

Celia the Cow then mooed again, stating her own hello, not wanting to feel left out.

"Hello Celia. Enjoying the weather?" Neil asked, chuckling at the sight he was seeing.

"She sure is," said the Man, "so much so that she wanted more space! Broke right through the fence. And her friends too!"

Three other cows were all at various points on the road.

Crow settled on Neil's shoulders. "It seems that we should help him."

He nodded, "Can we help you move them back in?"

"Kind of you for offering, but Celia only moves when she wants too. She will when she is done. I probably will wait too. Enjoy the day myself."

"Seems we need to go around," Crow said. She dashed upwards into the blue sky.

After a minute or two she landed again. "Just off to the left, we can go over a small creek and in front of those trees."

So they set off to the creek. Turning off the road, they went to the creek. Once there, they stopped. The creek seemed to be assuredly rushing this day.

The fall rain had it raise some few inches above where it should have been. Neil looked to his left. Then to the right.

No bridge in sight.

"There is no bridge," Neil said, frowning.

The Crow also clicked in disappointment. "We have to go around. I can't have your mother upset that you crossed a dangerous creek and getting wet no less!"

Neil took a moment to look at his surroundings. Mother always told him to see all his directions before he chose one.

"Look around you. The world is indeed beautiful but sometimes it takes a little longer to get where you are going. No need to rush. It gives you more time to enjoy what you are seeing."

He did just that. Just to his left, there were some tall, green trees lining the creek. An old tractor road wound its way through the bushes.

"There is a path to the woods there. It could lead to where we want to go."

"Oh I don't know; those look a bit dark. Aren't you afraid it'll be scary?"

To some it would spooky. Not Neil. He had his Crow, a friend. And Mother said that if he stood up good and tall, then nothing could scare him.

He straightened his back and puffed out his chest. "I am not scared."

The Crow landed on his shoulder, "Then let's be quick! We don't want to dally all day thinking about it."

Neil began to whistle a tune he heard his mother sing whenever she was walking out and about. It was a peppy one, one that would put a spring in any step as one put one foot forward.

Crow hummed it at the start, then she began to whistle as well as a crow could.

What a pair they made as they wandered down the dirt path, the sun at their backs. The dark trees were greeting them as they walked up. If Neil listened closely, he could hear the sounds of small animals bustling about in the bushes just out of sight.

As they stepped between the trees, the darkness happened upon them with no warning. The warm sun was now behind them.

The air became cool and a little damp.

The road started to wind away out of sight as the pair ventured off to wherever it led.

Chapter 4

As Neil and the Crow were exploring the dirt road they currently were walking on, the minutes were going by very slowly. They had approached a fork in the road.

"What way do you think we should go?" Neil asked.

There were two choices to pick from. Both made their own way through the dark trees without a hint to what the right direction to be chosen was.

At this point, despite the minutes ticking slowly by, it was known that they indeed had been traveling for some time, even if the sunlight hadn't changed overhead. Crow often tried to fly high and see what way to go, but the branches became too thick to see the path properly.

"I suppose we shall just pick one. We could always walk back if we feel we chose wrong," Crow said hopping down from Neil's shoulder, from where she had come to rest when not flying.

This stumped him. The path so far had been straight and fair, now it was playing games with them. How unfair for something they could not control, to be trifling with them.

"I bet we pick one better if we flip a coin. What do you say?"

"I say it seems as good as any idea I've got. You have a coin?"

Neil bit his lip and dug into his pockets. Out in his hand was a thimble, a toothpick, a loose button from a jacket he no longer wore, and some string.

"No. Now what?"

If Crows could frown, she did. "Take the thimble and the button in your hands and put them behind your back. The thimble is the left path. The button, the right. Shuffle them, and I will pick a hand. Whatever you show, that is what we choose."

Neil did this and took a moment to shuffle them around. "I'm ready. Which hand do you choose?"

"Left."

The left hand revealed the thimble.

"Left it is!" Neil was excited to be off once more.

Crow apparently felt the same. They marched off to the left path and sung some melodies to pass the time. After a time, it soon became obvious to Neil that the path looked just the same as the one they were previously on, and that they seemed to not be any closer to Mr. Dodson's.

The fact of the matter was, they were now lost. The path had wound and turned some, and there were some more forks they decided to take, he was quite sure of it. Or did they not?

Silly him. He could not remember.

"Crow?" Neil asked.

"Yes?" Crow replied in a sing song, birdlike melody.

"What do you suppose we would find in these woods if we were to leave the path?"

She slowed her singing and flapped her wings to get in front of him.

"Oh, I think we would find all sorts of things. Big things, scary things, wild things. I imagine it would contain dangerous things."

"Things we haven't seen before?"

"Why, maybe."

Neil hopped over a log on the ground and over a large mushroom sitting next to it. "I think it would be very fun to find something I ain't seen before. Besides, we have come to be lost anyways."

"Have never seen before. Don't use 'ain't'. Yes, I suppose it could be fun. Although I don't think it would be wise. Also, I'm not sure we are lost."

"Oh I highly recommend it if you have time," a deep almost rhythmic voice came from the bushes, "and if you do not know if you are lost, then surly you are indeed, lost."

Crow cawed in surprise and Neil leapt himself.

Crawling out from the bushes was a brown Tom Cat.

"Sorry to startle you, I mean no harm," he said, purring at the end. His eyes were a bright sunflower yellow with black retinas.

He had a long, mangy tail that was whipping back and forth. The bottom of the Tom's paws were dusty with some dirt, and his fur seemed to have gathered a leaf or two in his travels.

This cat had the look that he had been on the move for some time. Oh, the things he must have seen.

Mother Crow settled in front of Neil on the ground, fluttering her wings. "Of course. It was just the...shock of a new voice. We thought we were alone is all."

"Oh, but in these woods you can never be too sure."

The Tom shivered and stretched its back legs. "Forgive me, where are my manners? I'm Tom, adventurer extraordinaire. If you would like, I can offer my services as a guide through these parts."

If a cat could bow, surly Tom did so.

Neil reached out his hand, unsure what formality to do when approached by a gentlecat.

"My name is Neil. How do you do," Neil said.

"Quite well. Had a run in with some rough squirrels, but no harm done."

"Squirrels?"

The Tom laughed, "Oh yes, nasty sort. They wanted some of my coin. Sad for them, I have none!"

Crow hopped closer to the Tom, "And where did you see these squirrels? We shall try and avoid them."

The large brown cat casually walked in a circle around the two companions. To them, it seemed he was in no hurry to run if there was danger about.

"Don't worry about them. I was able to dissuade them from coming any further to the road. Which was the right idea. It saved you from having to deal with them by yourself."

"I think we would ought to have fared well," Neil said, squaring his shoulders.

"Yes, yes, of course. How silly of me. More right for them to avoid you, than the other way around."

"Well, we thank you for your help to save those poor souls," Crow chirped flying back to Neil's shoulder, "Sorry to cut this cheery meeting short, but we have time to keep."

The Cat laughed. "You can keep time? How curious. I must know how you do it."

"Perhaps some other time. Maybe when we cross paths again," Crow said, using her beak to nudge Neil into moving.

"Then as a thank you, maybe I follow for a bit? It has been a time since I had friends for an adventure. I assume you ARE adventuring, aren't you?"

"Of course!" Neil said excitedly, "We are going to Mr. Dodson's farm to gather some pumpkin seeds and pumpkins. You should come with us."

"Oh Neil, I don't think we could bother Mr. Tom with our-" Crow began. She was cut off by Tom, which, looking back could be seen as rather rude but at the time, if he were to get words in, than that was the best thing he could do.

"Nonsense. I won't slow you either. I know these woods like the back of my paw! And to pass the time, I also have stories!"

"Stories?"

"Oh yes," the Tom purred, slinking around once more, his bright eyes flashing, "from my travels. I've been everywhere exciting in these parts. Some not, but those have their place."

Neil thought back to what his mother said of stray cats, but it came fuzzy. All he could remember was this:

"Now, Neil, when you come across a stray, be kind and show them dignity. They wander, but often by choice. You can learn a thing or two from them but be careful."

"Why so Mother?"

"If it's one thing they do well, it is look out for themselves. But don't judge, they can also be quite the friend when you are in need."

From what this Tom Cat has shown, Neil saw no fear of him posing any sort of danger whatsoever. He would be glad to have two friends on this trip. Two! Could one imagine!

"Tom," Neil said, "could you help us get back to the right path? I think we're lost."

"Oh quite you are. I will do my best to ensure a safe travel to your beloved pumpkins. You have my word."

Neil was taught that someone's word was the best they can give.

The three began off once more down the path, humming a tune as the Tom lead the way, prancing back and forth from the front to the back.

Chapter 5

What a trio they made. Neil, walking bravely and happily, Tom sporadically trotting a few yards ahead, and Crow never leaving Neil's shoulder, whistling a tune to keep the steps light and free.

Little care was taken to the slow dropping light, and the increasing overgrowth of the bushes and low-hanging branches of the trees. This went on until Neil had to squint to see more than a few feet in front of him. Counting the number of people in the party, he realized that Tom was nowhere to be see.

"Crow, can you see Tom? It is really dark. Why, I can't see a thing," said Neil.

"I agree. All quite menacing. I don't see that Cat at all. Where has he gone off too?"

They both called out to see if he was nearby.

"Oh, I hope he hasn't ran off. He was supposed to lead us to the end of this trail."

"He did give his word that he would...look! Lights."

He pointed and there were two glowing lights. It was all fairly unnerving. Crow flapped down in front of Neil and cawed at them.

They blinked. Tom came walking from the dark. "I have a habit of startling you don't I. I was wondering why you had stopped following me."

Crow bristled, "We can't see a thing in these shadows."

"So it seems. Perhaps I know someone who can help. This fellow I know sells lantern flowers, they may help your eyes since they aren't like mine," as he said this, he blinked his beautiful golden eyes, causing them to shine on and off.

"I think we have taken long enough, but a light would be welcomed," Crow said, looking up at Neil.

"A light would speed up things. But what is a...lantern flower? I have never heard of that."

The Tom laughed, "It is exactly as it sounds. A flower that grows here, and only here, it gives off a glow like a lantern. Unfortunately, it grows in certain parts here. One is close by though, where my friend harvests them."

So they followed their guide as he led them onward.

Neil heard his stomach make a low rumbling noise.

"Tom?"

"Hmmmm?" Tom replied lazily walking this way and that in a zig-zag path ahead of them.

"You don't suppose we can find something to eat?" he looked at Crow, "I haven't anything to eat since breakfast."

Tom pranced to his hind legs to the side of a tree, "Then it is lunch!"

"And what shall we eat?" Crow said, skeptical.

The Tom laughed, his whiskers turning upward in a smile while he got down from the tree. "Don't sound so negative Crowy Girl. We will find some food just up ahead. My harvester friend can find some."

"Where is this friend of yours?" Crow asked.

The Tom flicked his tail, "Remember that creek back a way? It is the same one...just around this bend here."

The small group came up to a well-kept lawn of river grass, a wood cabin with a rocking chair on the porch, and a dock with a rowboat set on the creek that had widened enough to be called a river. A brown railed fence was set up throughout the lawn, marking the end or start of the place. Depending on if you were coming or going.

Fireflies buzzed around the property, dashing this way and that, free to do as they pleased.

The Tom pranced up and over the fence, making his way to the porch.

"Oh Mr. Trinket! Mr. Trinket, you have guests for some lanterns! Mr. Trinket." Tom was pawing the front door of the cabin.

It opened to show an older man, with a wide brimmed hat and a cigar sticking out of the right side of his mouth. Mr. Trinket had a light gray beard, frizzled, and frazzled, with no order.

He was wearing a pair of brown fishing pants, galoshes, and a blue plaid shirt.

Grinning to show a row of bright teeth, Mr. Trinket waved his hands.

"Howdy Tom! Lanterns you say, eh? I fer' sure got those some'weres. Howdy, young man. Ma'am."

He tipped his hat and sauntered off the porch, hands in his pants pockets.

"Hello, thanks for helping us." Neil offered his hand. He found that handshakes were a good way to say thank you.

The hand of Mr. Trinket was warm and rough, most likely from the years he had spent farming lantern flowers.

"Oh, no, thank you. Always happy to see a guest. How many you think you'll need?"

Neil rubbed his chin. "I think one aught to do it. Unless, Crow, did you need one?"

Crow shuffled her feathers. "Two. I certainly can't carry one but it would be a wise choice to have one in case something happens to the first."

The man nodded, "Wise indeed. Don't want to find yerself stuck in the dark without a light. Things can get sticky if you do," he took out and put back his cigar after puffing some woody smoke, "Now, if yer would follow me."

He made his way to the dock house situated next to the rowboat.

"Why the boat?" Crow asked.

Tom was on his haunches near the boat, "His field is close by, but down the creek."

"Right, you would know all about that, wouldn't ya, Tom?" Mr. Trinket said as he reached down to rub his chin.

He waved them into his dock-house. On the walls, there were fishing lines and hooks, situated with lures of all kinds. A few knives and saws hung from the rafter. On the wall was the frightening face of an unknown animal. It was snarling and its teeth were barred.

Crow yelped and flew a short distance back in shock. Neil also was startled by the ugly sight.

Mr. Trinket laughed, "Don't you be afraid. I only thought it would be honorable to pin him up and show how great he was."

It was a vicious looking thing. A thing that neither Neil, nor Crow, nor Tom had ever seen before.

"Vile creature," Tom said, "what is it?"

Mr. Trinket moved his hat up and then down. "It is a Teethersnatch. Not common but I find 'em around the woods on my way to my lantern farm."

Crow shuffled nervously, "There...there are more of those around? Are they dangerous?"

"Wouldn't be on my wall if they weren't!" Mr. Trinket laughed as he picked up an oar, "Now, let us be off to get you your lanterns!"

The three companions all looked at one another as they followed the boatman to his dock. Even though they would have liked to move onward without the sights they had seen in the cabin, it was well known that they could not do so without the lamps.

They supposed they would have to trust the boatman, even if danger seemingly lurked at every corner in this particular spot in the woods.

"Everyone ready?" Their boatman asked.

Everyone nodded.

"Off we go, please keep hands and legs and heads in the boat at all times."

The boat was a curious thing. A lamp hanging from a crooked pole was at the front and two benches were built into the sides in the heart of it. There was room for everyone, but in a snug fashion.

A light mist set in over the group as their Boatman used a large wooden pole to push them from the dock.

Off they went.

Chapter 6

A cool breeze swallowed the boating party as they made their way through the water. Now, never having been on many boats, Neil felt funny. It was the same feeling he got when he ate too much of his Mother's Winter soup.

"Crow," Neil whispered in the musty fog.

"Yes Neil?" Crow whispered back. It was as if they wished to not have the boatman hear them. Currently, he indeed was having a light conversation with the Tom Cat. Fearing that being offered a ride to the lantern farm had made him sick, Neil believed it was rude to say so, seeing it was a nice gesture.

Mother had always told him that if he had nothing nice to say, then he shouldn't say it at all.

But he could not help himself. He did feel awfully ill.

"I feel sick. I fear I may be seasick. My uncle used to talk of that sort of thing when he was a fisherman."

"Oh dear, maybe we could ask him to slow down a bit. We're going a tad fast for my liking."

"Don't birds like to fly fast? I know I would."

"Oh not Crows. We like to enjoy the flight as we go. If we must go fast we shall, but we ought to enjoy the world while we can."

"That sounds awfully like something an owl would say. Wouldn't you think?"

"Well, I said they are pretentious. Not wrong."

"Don't tell them to stop. They seem to be enjoying themselves. Besides, we must be almost there."

"Sir!" Crow said, "Are we almost there? I dare say I feel chilly in this mist."

"Oh, can we tell if we are anywhere?" he replied.

The Tom laughed.

"I must confess, I don't know what you are saying."

"Can you not know? Or do you simply not truthfully see?"

"See?"

"The funniness about it!"

Crow began to shift nervously. She very well could smell the air full of something. Then she saw the bottle lying about the bottom. It was no wonder that Neil was sick. They had taken to a bottle of some strong drink no doubt!

"You drank something, didn't you?" Crow asked, backing up to her charge slowly, almost without notice.

Tom was rolling on the bottom of the boat, licking his paws.

"Oh, come now! It is some nice pumpkin spiced drink. Having a bit of fun isn't wrong, is it?"

"it most certainly can be when we are on the water!"

"Oh, come now. No more whining. We are here aren't we?"

So they were. Neil and Crow stepped out of the boat to see a small field lined with stemmed, white flowers. Another cabin was standing near the dirt landing.

Tom hopped out and continued to clean himself.

"Tom, you too?"

He gazed at her; his eyes were milky.

She cawed at him and flapped up to Neil's shoulder.

They followed the man as he wandered to the cabin.

"Just a moment. Have yer'self a look for a few lanterns, I have to ge' summthin to get them ta' glow."

The two of them made their way through the flowers and came across several they like.

After choosing three, sturdy lanterns, Neil was able to pluck them quite easily.

The man came out from the cabin, holding a plain, clay jar. He had removed his cap and now was frowning at them, although it was hard to tell in the dim light from the boat. For that was the only light they had, sifting, and weaving its way through the misty air. The illusion it created was that of a dark and rainy night, except there was no rain to be had.

"Sir, we were able to select a few for you to light."

"Why did you pick 'em? I didn't say ya could pick 'em."

His voice was low and hoarse.

"I'm so sorry. Have we ruined them?" Neil asked, "I thought it would be easier to bring them to you in the dark, to light it easier."

"Oh, so ye' be farmers, right? Know your way around my lanterns, right?"

"Neil," Crow cawed as she tugged at his shirt to get to the woods.

"Sir I-"

He hissed.

"Tom!" Crow shouted. The man was advancing quicker and quicker. Tom blinked and shook his head.

"What would you like me to do? You're the one who plucked without asking! How rude!" Tom the Cat just licked his paws.

"Now, let me show you how I light my lanterns!" He pulled a bright knife, glistening in the mist. Neil had wondered what was in the jar. That sick feeling he had earlier returned when he could guess what it was.

Crow squawked at the man and flapped her wings madly in his face to distract him. He tossed his arms about, trying to shoo her away.

She poked at his face, then his eyes, and finally pulled some hair out of his beard.

The Tom shook off whatever was ailing him and began to whine.

Neil thought there was no way they could be caught if Mr. Trinket could not see.

So he very clumsily made his way to the lanterns on the boat and tried to blow them out.

When he could not, then he pulled them out and threw them on the ground.

With a large noise, the whole area went dark without the lanterns to keep it away.

Crow nudged Neil in the direction she thought was the woods and they both stumbled their way into them.

The boatman was wailing about his beard, not chasing. The Tom Cat was crying about being left behind, despite being able to see in the dark.

The whole scene was a mess of tears and bumbling through lost sentences.

After the commotion was a way's off, a small sliver of light peeked through the dark, no longer any mist to contend with.

It was clear at this point that the two had lost a dear amount of time chasing a cat to find some magical lanterns that proved to be not useful.

So they again were lost in the woods with little ways of being able to see.

Chapter 7

While Neil was catching his breath, Crow fluttered this way and that, trying to find the right way to go. To her, it was useless. Wandering so far off the right path had certainly led them down the one that was sure to get them more lost than found.

Little talk had gone on as she flew, muttering to herself. Most of this was about how she knew they should have talked Tom into staying on the path. Another point she made to herself was to never have followed him in the first place.

Although, this was harder to ponder since he HAD guided when they needed him the most. If it weren't for him, they would be further lost still.

Now the woods were dark and quiet. Not a bird was to be heard, not a howl of a dog, nor the shuffling of a mouse.

It seemed the more they tried to get to the heralded pumpkin path, the farther away from it they were getting.

Running from the excitement back at the boatmen's property, Neil had forgotten all about being hungry, but the feeling had returned.

"Oh dear, oh dear, it seems we are lost again Neil."

"Don't worry Crow, we shall find a way. I do see it is rather sad how that all turned out. And I still am hungry."

The Crow shuttered her wings. Searching the ground, she found some moss. "I don't suppose you eat worms do you?"

He shook his head.

"Well, here, try some of this moss. I hear it can be good for you."

Reluctantly, he did so. It was soft and spongy, and picking the dirt out, he was able to swallow it. Although it was nice to eat something, it wouldn't starve off the hunger much longer.

"Hello! Hello there!" A high-pitched voice sounded from above. Within a few seconds, they were greeted by a large, dark brown Owl swooping in from the skies.

"Hello," replied Neil.

The Owl reached out a large wing, "I was wondering if you could offer me direction, I am aiming to get out of these unforgiving woods."

Crow shook his wing, "So are we, sad to say. Sorry we couldn't help you. We had a bad experience with someone offering to help."

The Owl blinked its very large eyes, "Well thankful for you, I am not asking to help. I need it myself. I pose no harm unless you are a mouse. As you can see, I am large enough to fend for myself."

Crow and Neil looked at the other.

Crow was the first to respond, "Now, I know owls keep their words to the highest end. If you gave us yours that your intent is true, then we will offer any assistance we can to get out of these woods together!"

The Owl hooted, "Of course, of course. So long as you return the favor."

They each reached out a wing and flapped them together. Neil assumed this was the same as him shaking someone else's hand.

Once that was accomplished, the Owl introduced himself as Oslo. Once the formalities were exchanged and each knew the name of the other, they began to discuss the way they should go.

Then he saw the Neil was putting moss in his mouth.

"What on earth are you doing, dear boy?"

Neil was surprised, "Eating moss."

"And who gave you that idea? If you are hungry, you should eat some acorns, they are everywhere. Or mushrooms. They make a good stew."

Crow muttered to herself.

"No matter," he flapped his great big wings and disappeared into the dark. After a few seconds, he returned with a mouthful of several nut-like objects.

"Soft nuts. Easy to bite into. Go ahead."

Neil did so, they were soft and a little hard to chew but better than the moss. He smiled.

With that sorted and a few nuts left, they went back to discussing which way to head next.

Crow was insistent that they continue straight, until at least they come to another fork in the road.

Neil thought they should go to the left.

Oslo offered the suggestion of going to the right.

What was not under debate, was going back the way they came.

After telling Oslo their ordeal with the boatman and the Tom Cat, he shuttered his feathers and agreed that they should not go back.

"Oh, you followed a cat? Those darn things can either be the best of companions or look out only for themselves. I feel sorry it was the latter. You should have been more thorough though with whom you trust." He said the word 'whom' with a long and drawn out 'o' sound, hooting as owls tend to do.

"We needed the help and he seemed a rather nice fellow," Neil said, crossing his arms.

The Owl ruffled his wings. "Well, I'm a nice fellow and you are choosing to trust me, how do you know that I am not wanting to lead you away?"

This was a question that had Neil thinking on the right answer. What the large bird said was true. They trusted the Tom Cat and it failed to help them. Why would trusting the Owl turn out any different?

Crow spoke up, "One, you are not rather nice, you are quite the opposite. Secondly, I have known many owls in my life and none have ever had hidden motives or ideas against what they say."

The Owl laughed, "How do YOU…" he swiveled his head up and down, "know so many owls? Crows don't meet owls often."

Crow squawked. "I have traveled a lot and gone many places, thank you very much."

"And that they don't deceive?"

"They are too pompous and arrogant to do so. By believing they are always in the right and so ever wise, they see no reason to hide their outstanding qualities."

This silenced the Owl for a moment, or two. He was unsure of how to respond to a bird lower on the food chain speaking out to him like this. Perhaps the Crow was right. Maybe he WAS being a tad too pompous for his own good. Never though, would he admit that. He already had admitted to being lost; it was too much to admit acting in a rude manner. The reputation he held would be tarnished. And that was something he could not allow to happen.

"Well, then I know this: we should continue in a straight direction that you were heading and see if I can find a good alternative in the meantime."

That was as close to an apology the group was going to get.

And so they were off once more. What was to come, they did not know, but they would all face it together if something were to happen.

Chapter 8

Time passed in what seemed like days for the three traveling companions. None dared to point that out however, out of fear to sadden the others at their apparent lack of progress.

That was, until they happened upon what seemed like a clearing in the woods. The path they were walking on continued through a great big hedge. And coming through the hedge were rays of what they hoped was sunlight.

It was quiet on their journey, for idle chit chat had grown silent. No other travelers or critters were to be seen or heard nearby. If it were not for the company of the two, Neil was unsure if he would have been able to continue onward.

He guessed that was what his Mother meant when she told him thus: "Pleasant company always makes dull moments better."

Crow would object and say that the Owl was not pleasant in any shape, but Neil found him quite agreeable to travel with. He was smart, certainly, but his jokes often made Neil laugh, despite their dryness.

Cynical is how one could describe the Owl. Finding things that could go wrong was his specialty it seemed. The unusual situation was that although things could go wrong, Owl always pitched a solution to make it right, granting him a funny balance between optimism and pessimism.

And so they found themselves stopping and staring at the hedge before them.

"What do you suppose lies behind it?" Neil asked, not taking his eyes off of the behemoth.

"Could not be worse than what we already have encountered," said Crow, who was perched on his shoulder.

"I imagine any number of things. Some good. Some bad."

"What a sterling report," Crow said.

Owl huffed his feathers. "I was only pointing out that we don't know what to see but it appears," Owl said as he turned his head to Neil almost behind him, "I imagine whatever lies beyond this hedge, we must see if we want to go any farther."

All three nodded to themselves and Neil led the way to push branches of the hedge out of the way.

What lied beyond was a large opening, the edges of which were not seen.

In the middle was a pond of sparkling blue water. A hummingbird whirred by them as it flew to a nearby flower.

Sunlight was everywhere, making the whole place warmer than the woods they had just come from.

It had been an awfully long journey for them. Maybe a rest or two would be good for their health.

Even Crow agreed to this.

At first, she was object. "I think we should…my it IS warm and cozy here, isn't it?"

The Owl was already making his way to the water's edge. Several large plants had enormous leaves hanging from them. They created small patches of cool shade for them to lie under.

"It IS! And what a water source. It is so clear I can see my own face," Neil said softly. He peered into the water as it rippled gently against the soft bank. His own face was smiling back at him. He couldn't remember himself smiling at it, however.

Perhaps he was and not realized how relaxed he was.

Mother always told him to not question a good thing too often. If you do that, then you could lose being happy when it is there.

Instead, he took off his shoes and waded into the clear water. The water was cooler than the air, but not so much so that made it uncomfortable. Across the edges of the water were small lily pads with a flower raising out of each. They were white in color with rounded tips. Each one seemed to sway in the breeze, creating a mist of their pollen. It was like a grand painting.

Crow bustled in the water and cleaned her wings. Neil laid back under a large lily leaf. The Owl soared all around the area, enjoying spreading his large wings after such a long walk.

They were enjoying themselves.

What they could not see was the several things watching them beyond the sunshine. The light faded off without a clear border and the trail back to the woods left unnoticed.

Chapter 9

It was Neil who first understood that something had gone terribly, terribly, wrong. Waking from a nap, he rubbed his eyes and yawned. As he did so, he noticed that both Owl and Crow had also fallen asleep. This was nothing unusual as it was a very comforting place.

After a time on the road, resting was needed but as he wakened he felt something was off.

Mother had always told him to trust his intuition. It was never wrong if given the proper trust.

He noticed three things.

The first was that both Crow and Owl were sleeping, making the whole pond area eerily quiet. This should have been louder, maybe another singing songbird or two.

The second thing he noticed was that the water was no longer moving. It was almost completely still. He was no expert in the ways of water, but he did know enough that it should be moving in some kind.

The third was that there was no warmth coming from the sunshine anymore. It was as cold as it was in the middle of winter, he crossed his arms and shivered.

The worst part of it, was he was still tired even since he was sure he had slept a very long time.

He wondered what his mother would do.

The first thing he was sure, was that she would wake her friends.

"Crow! Owl!" Neil said, his voice low and scratchy.

Neither Crow, nor Owl stirred.

He tried again, this time forcing himself to shout. It still came out as if he were talking in a whisper.

This time, both birds woke with a startle.

Fluttering his wings, the Owl blinked his large eyes several times and turned his head around and around, back, and forth.

"My, oh my! What has happened?" Crow said, waddling across the low grass to Neil.

"I do believe, my dear companions, that we have been exposed to...are there small, blue mushrooms near where you took a slumber?"

Both Neil and Crow glanced down. Indeed, there were small blue bulbs rising from the ground. They nodded.

"Oh dear, seems we have been exposed to Whisper 'Shrooms. Ate them even, in our delightful hunger. They are called as such as they make you seem groggy and speak in low tones. But that isn't the worst."

He grew silent.

Crow was the first to break it, "What is worse?"

"Where they grow and who eats them. They make you lose track of time in order for their Harvesters to capture you. Fortunately for us, they have not the same effect as others."

"I would not be so sure," Neil said as he watched little grey creatures slowly creep their way into the grass. They were larger than rabbits, but not as big as dogs. They were quiet and had small back feet, and large, clawed front paws.

Neil looked around the ground. He sought something defend himself. His mother always taught him stand up for himself and this was no time to argue that lesson.

He found a limp piece of stem from the large plants that he had slept under. It would have to do.

As one jumped at him, he swung the stem as fast as he could. It hit the Harvester and it turned away. The rest stopped and then pounced at Owl.

Owl then flapped his mighty wings and kept the things away. They did not want to test his strength.

Crow flew in and out of the crowd of Harvesters and was able to poke several in the face, driving them mad and turning them away.

"Oslo!" Crow shouted, "We must get to the woods where can lose them in the dark!"

"Agreed!" he shouted back.

With that they made their way longer and longer paths to and from the pack of hungry Harvesters.

Neil swung his stem wildly. He hit a few, but the most effective thing to happen, was that they were too afraid to get clubbed with it so they stayed at arm's length.

The three travelers managed to reach the woods line without anything more than being tired.

Scrambling over a few low-lying branches, Neil tripped over one and snagged his pants.

He tugged at them and got them off, but on one leg they tore a hole. His mother would be disappointed to have to sew a new pair so early, but he guessed it would be fine since he would not be eaten by those Mushroom Harvesters.

As he pulled himself upwards to be able to run, Oslo was able to fend off their attackers. Crow bit into Neil's shirt and did her best to help drag him away.

After a few tense minutes where there was screeching and confusion of Crow and Oslo swooping this way and that, to distract the Harvesters, the three were able to get far enough away to not fear their sharp teeth or immense claws.

Without further words they dashed away into the woods, further into the descending darkness.

Chapter 10

It had been sometime since any member of the group had said anything more than a mumble about not looking back or a panted breath.

Neil began to grow tired. It seemed to him that he never went to sleep at all. Perhaps he was still dreaming, or that sleeping was a dream.

What he did know was that his two friends had an endless supply of energy and power.

Being a bird of prey seemed like a wonderous thing. Being able to be close to the sky, flying through the endless blue ocean-like sky without having to slow down for anyone or anything.

But he was not a bird. He was only Neil. He had been told that it was enough, but at the current time, he felt it was not. Unable to fly, he could not see what was ahead, unable to sleep, he was doomed to walk in a haze with a lack of attention.

What a poor sight he was. His mother would disapprove he was sure of it.

For the longest time he was happy to walk in silence. He had nothing to say anyhow.

Crow would let him know if anything were to happen. Perhaps he could sleepwalk.

Crow spoke up to mess with his thoughts.

"I think there is something up ahead just there. A light."

Oslo shook himself out of the daze they all seemed to be in. "What...oh yes...a light. That has worked for us recently."

Crow squawked, "Please Oslo. Let us try and be happy. Not all is lost."

Neil could argue that point. However, he only stopped walking and sat down against a stone that was resting on the side of their path.

"What is wrong, young Neil?" Oslo asked, turning his head around to observe.

Neil said nothing. He was too tired to answer.

Crow flew down beside him and wrapped her wings around him. "It is OK. I shall go ahead and see what is there, you rest. You have been through a lot."

"Indeed. I will watch the boy," the Owl said. He stood in front of him and kept watch. The empty path was quiet except Neil, who slowly began to fall asleep. The last thing he saw as his vision faded, was the outline of Crow as she fluttered away. If a bird could have a concerned look on their face, she had one.

Over the course of the next period of time, Neil faded in and out and he saw glimpses of a tall figure scooping him into the air.

Sounds were distant and quiet. The voices he heard were muffled. He could hear Crow chirping now and then, from where he could not tell.

She did not seem too concerned that he was being moved. Nor did Oslo. With that justification, he dozed off to sleep.

When he awoke next, he was lying down. Something was poking into his side and a spot itched on his legs. He scratched it only to feel a light stick prodding his fingers.

He sat slowly, rubbing the sides of his head.

He looked at what was prodding him and saw a faint colored yellow piece of straw.

It seemed Neil had been placed onto a mattress made solely of the dried plant.

Stretching his legs, he yawned and looked about the room.

Crow was perched on a small wooden chair next to the bed, her beak nestled into her wing.

The room he was in, well, no more than a hut really, was brown and yellow. It was seemingly made of the same straw as his itchy bed.

There was a crude painting on one point of the circled room. Sided on the end of his bed there was a wooden structure that when, on closer inspection, was a three drawered dresser.

The dirt floor had a thick woolen rug next to bed side. Some wooden toys lay strewn about to one side with a small table with a small chair in the middle of the space.

The missing chair must have been what Crow had been resting on.

Neil furred his brow and clenched his teeth, the things he did when he thought hard about something.

Trying to remember what had happened to him was doing him no good.

Every time he thought about it, his eyes went fuzzy and he gained a headache.

Such a person who had never drank an ounce of alcohol could not know what being hungover was, but surly that is what he was feeling.

Even Neil knew that something made him sick after they tried to doze off near the lake.

Bits and pieces of information were there.

He then did an exercise to see if he was seriously injured.

The first thing he could remember was walking into the woods with Crow and meeting the Tom Cat shortly after. The Tom had led to them his 'friend' Mr. Trinket the Boatmen. He shivered at the thought, not wanting to think about what might have been if he and Crow had not been able to escape.

The next thing he tried to remember was walking along a few forks in the road, where Crow thought they had made some wrong turns.

Now, looking back, he believed she was right. After that was a blurred account.

The next thing his mind was able to find out was...nothing.

He had woken up here in the straw bed and that was that.

After he saw movement in the corner of his eye he jumped.

It was gone out the sliding door of the hut.

He tip-toed there, careful not to wake Crow, who was sound asleep. He was sure that she needed as much sleep as he did.

Taking a breath he slid open the door.

Chapter 11

What awaited Neil when he stepped from the hut was nothing what he imagined.

He found himself not on a dirt road, but one that was filled of cobblestone and river pebbles. Packed nice and neat, it made a smooth walking surface. Nor was he the only thing out on the path.

Walking this way and that were people. Ordinary people dressed in a variety of clothes, but they were colorful, nonetheless. From reds to yellow to some dark greens, Neil saw more colors than he could imagine.

Most were wearing a hat of some kind to block out the now bright sunlight. It was the first time in a long while that he remembered what the sun felt like. It was warm and soothing.

He took a deep breath and felt the fresh air take its wanted effect.

Huts and small buildings made of stone were beautifully built and placed along the road on either side. Lamps that were made of what looked like dried corn husks were on poles set behind a red wooden fence that lined the road, buildings set were behind.

When he stepped to the road, he was able to get a closer look at these people wandering down it. Every now and then they would hesitate and take a look at him, then smile or wave.

Seeing someone confused on their road must not have been odd.

What was odd, however, was what Neil saw when they smiled. They were…orange.

They had something that looked rougher than skin but he was unsure what he could compare it too.

The most interesting thing he saw was their eyes. They were pitch black. He had never seen such things.

His own eyes widened when he heard Crow behind him. At the sound of her caw, he jumped into the air.

"Oh! Sorry to scare you. I meant to only ask how you are."

He hugged himself. "No, that is OK. Crow, what on earth is this place?"

She flapped and flew to his shoulder. She put a wing around his neck, "I think it is a town of some kind. Or village. Oslo came back with a tall fellow in a straw hat. He picked you up after you had passed out. We were quite concerned and worried that this fellow may have had ill intentions, but he only wanted to help."

"And what of Oslo?"

"He is around somewhere. Some time ago he wandered off babbling on about help or a doctor of some kind. I haven't seen him since. Although, I did fall asleep as you did."

Neil shuddered. He was having his fill of unusual sights and meeting unusual people.

"Crow…" he paused, "have you noticed…well…I don't want to be rude but…"

"Yes. I noticed. I have heard of such things but I hadn't believed until now."

"Heard of what things?

"Sometimes, those who live and work closely with the land take on parts of the land. Here, it means –"

"It means," a high-pitched voice spoke next to them, "that since we harvest pumpkins and squash of all kinds, as well as other fall foods, we have turned orange!"

Crow and Neil turned to see Oslo standing next to a Falling person, one who was smiling a dark, toothless smile but with a cheery demeanor.

"Oh, hello sir. I meant nothing by it."

"No problem at all my young fellow. I suppose it could be quite shocking for those not used to unusual things."

"Well, we have had our fair share of unusual the last few…however long it has been."

It was the Falling man's turn to have a confused look, "You don't know how long you have been traveling? My new friend Oslo here has informed me that you had a brush with some peculiar mushrooms."

Both of them nodded their respective heads.

He clapped his straw-colored hands together. "Well, I cannot help you with what you lost but I can help with where you go from here. I am sure that this is the safest place you have been for some time, regardless of how long that 'sometime' has been."

With that said he turned and led the trio down the well-made road to a larger hut in the middle of a larger circle of road.

"This is the town hall," he said as he waved his hand toward the large building, "we will get you something warm to eat before you meet our town leader."

The three were staring at the large town hall. It was really impressive to all of them. None had seen such a thing. The entire day was one of new things to see and hear. There were many more people around this part of the village.

It was a wonder of just how this existed in the forest. It was big and magical, and hidden from everything unless you knew about it.

For Neil, who was not as young as he was before going into the woods, this was something he would always remember.

Heading into the building, the guide led them to a big table in an oblong shape.

They each sat in a lovely wooden chair and had plates of steaming food placed in front of them.

"I hate to be rude, but what did we do to get this great meal?" Oslo said.

Crow and Neil both stopped when they realized they were already eating.

The guide laughed, "We simply thought you all could use a good meal after traveling so long. Good manners come second nature to us."

It was good enough. They dug in.

The large meal had a warm roast turkey, pumpkin pudding, cranberries, steamed vegetables, sliced bread, and a variety of fruits.

Hungrier than he ever had been, Neil could feel the hearty meal satisfy him.

Once the meal was picked over, they all drunk it down with some warm cider. A perfect end to a perfect meal.

They were then able to get a better look at the room they were in.

It was a very large, circular place, matching what was on the outside. The table was the center of it, with a door every few yards or so along the wall. The food had come out from what was guessed to be the kitchen.

Lamps scattered the wall to give the room light. They contained flames that danced within the glass cases.

Other than that, the fall-colored room was simply decorated, similar to that of the room Neil had woken up in.

They talked and were curious about what was behind all the doors. Not wanting to be rude, they decided to not to explore until permission was given.

That was a good idea as the guide who led them to the table came out of one of the closed doors, along with two stern looking guards, each holding a spear like object.

"I would introduce our town chief Frieda."

The guide bowed and stepped away to reveal a woman dressed in a yellow and red dress, with a green stripe wandering in random patterns on the front.

She looked similar to Neil but retained the tall-like quality like the rest of the townsfolk.

Frieda the Chief smiled. When she spoke, her voice sounded like the other folk.

"Hello there, it is a pleasure to meet travelers. We get several but none that have created a stir like you."

"And how have we got such buzz around us?" Crow asked, hopping closer to Neil.

"Nothing wrong if that is what you ask. We simply have not met anyone who has come back from the Trinket farm nor the mushroom field and kept their minds about them," she glanced down at Neil, "it is quite impressive."

"Thank you," Neil said, returned the look. For how he noticed how tall she was, he seemed to be tall himself. Now that was an odd thing.

"I see you have finished eating. And must have several questions for me."

Oslo bustled his feathers, "I assume you know the answers?"

"Oslo! Be kind," Crow chided.

Frieda laughed, "It is fine. Yes, I have the answers you are looking for."

"See? She says she has the answers. We have a right to know."

"You have a right to be nicer to our hosts or I will see to it I peck out your best feathers when you fly!"

"Why…I…you cannot!" Oslo was taken aback and then the two began to chirp faster than either Frieda or Neil could understand.

So they had a conversation themselves.

"You have had quite the adventure, or so the miss Crow has told me," Freida said.

Neil nodded, "Filled with things I rather did not enjoy."

She motioned her hand towards his companions, who were still bickering back and forth, "It cannot be all that bad, can it?"

"No, I guess not."

"I also suppose you know that you have gotten older since you have been here?"

"What do you mean? I'm the age I always am...aren't I?" He looked down at himself. He did not feel any different.

"Oh? When you came in, did you not think that the table was a normal size, not overly big?"

"I guess it seems normal to me."

"And a while ago, it would have seemed larger. Have you seen a mirror today?"

Neil shook his head.

Frieda clapped her hands and someone brought a large silver mirror. "Look."

He did. He was older. By a few years it appeared. When did that happen?

"I imagine it was a mixture of the mushrooms and all the time in the dark you spent. You can't tell how old you are if you cannot see anything."

He thought on that. It made sense. He tried very hard to remember just when he and Crow entered the woods before they met the Tom Cat.

He came up with no time.

"I cannot think when we came here."

"Indeed. The same happened to me when I first came here."

Neil widened his eyes. Frieda was like him! That would explain why she hadn't took to the crops like the farmers. He assumed it was because she was busy ruling, not farming. It was because she started out like Neil. How interesting.

Frieda laughed. "Yes, I came to the woods as much as you did. Then again, I had no choice."

"What do you mean?"

"Do you like stories?"

He nodded.

"Very well. Would your friends like to hear it?"

Suddenly the squabbling of the two birds stopped. Both looked on the two and agreed in unison.

It was settled. They were to hear the story of Queen Frieda.

Chapter 12

"Now, the first thing you have to understand, was that it was many years ago when this all occurred. Your parents were not born yet. Including yours, Oslo, despite however old you are about to tell me you are.

"The woods here are very different from when I first came. It was a much brighter, happier place for the creatures to live in. Birds were more prevalent than they are now, as you noticed they are rather sparse. So too the woodland creatures that used to run wild.

"Why that is, we are not entirely sure. I think it has something to do with those blasted Harvesters. Clever little things. Nasty bunch though, as you know. It took a while, but they came first in small numbers, then in packs. Then those numbers grew to the point where we had fight to keep them in their own groves.

"We have managed to get them under control, but for how long concerns me.

"Yes. Back to my personal story. That is why you are here. I mention the Harvesters only because they did not exist when I arrived, but shortly after.

"My home was near a small town set next to a river. This river was busy with traffic of all sizes of boats. Most carried goods back and forth from other towns, but some did carry travelers, such as yourselves.

"One of these travelers was part of a traveling circus. When I was a teenager, me and my brother were near the dock where the boat arrived. Mother and father told us to be careful of the water. I was but my brother was not.

"He was trying to catch a red fish when he slipped off the dock and into the water. I was lying in the grass some ways away when I heard the splash.

"Before I could get there, a man jumped from the boat to rescue him in a brave act. The water was rushing that day, which is the reason why my parents told me to be mindful.

"My brother was not a very good swimmer. So I said every prayer I was taught to make sure he was well. The man was the answer. Or so I thought at the time.

"He was able to rescue my brother and brought him to shore. I was so grateful to the young man.

"I told him as much and he said he was never more pleased to help. We told him that we would find a way to pay him back, but he would have none of that sort of talk.

"Instead, he told us the best way to thank him was gather a certain type of plant from the woods and bring it to him at his camp. We asked him what type of plant it was, and he described it.

"The plant, he said, was very short, but easy to spot, due to its light blue color. Almost like a blue bell flower. The difference was that it looked like a rose from a distance but was more like a sunflower up close.

"Now, we explained to him that no such flower grew around the river. Laughing at that, he told us that it was something uncommon but he said it grew deep in the woods just beyond our home.

"He would have gone himself, he said, but he was far too busy setting up for the coming show. He was the one who built the camps you see.

"We asked him what he needed such a flower for, and he mentioned that someone he cared about was ill and that the flower could cure them.

"In debt to the young man, my brother was quick to accept the task. I, on the other hand, was hesitant. Our parents had told us stories about the goings-on in the woods. Some was good, some was bad. My worry was not finding the flower, I was sure we could find something so different, but my worry was that we would find ourselves lost and not able to get back home for dinner safely.

"In those days, I was the girl who would second guess many a thing, and I did second guess but not well enough it seems. A wise man once told me that remembering the past as it should have been, not as it actually was, would drive one quite mad. I would do well to remember that advice more often, as I think what occurred just that day.

"How I never wanted to meet that young who forced us to go do his deed. See? I am getting flustered, so I must take a breath and not get ahead of myself. My tale is half over, so I plead patience with my recollection. It is difficult to me.

"Once my brother convinced me to go after the traveler's flower, we packed some food from our home, in case we got hungry. Our parents were gone you see, out working. We expected to be back at dinner time, but we were to skip a mid-day meal so we wanted to be sure to take something to eat with us.

"As we ventured off to our task, our spirits were good and not much is to be told of us walking through the woods.

"The heart of my story comes once we got far enough down the trail, when my fears came true.

"Indeed, we found a grove where the blue sunflower grew, only to find that we had gone so far off the previously made trail. We had forgotten our parents warning to not stray. Me and my brother were quite lost.

"The flower itself was just as the young man described it. Once we picked enough to have an armful, we gathered our thoughts and went on our way. It was horribly the wrong way.

"Now, of course, we didn't know that at the time. We were under the impression all was well.

"So we continued on our way, talking and laughing back and forth about what we were to do once we arrived back home.

"As I say this, you must excuse the tears welling in my eyes, the next segment of the story is quite hard for me to tell.

"I lost my brother you see. Before you assume the worst, we were split up. I had stopped to find something to eat after a long journey. Our food we brought had ran out some time before.

"I was digging around some promising looking moss when he ventured off. To this very day, I know not why he did that. One moment he was looking for me, the next he states he had seen some food some distance back. I never saw him again.

"If I had reacted better I would have gone with him. Yet, I was content in finding my own food. It had been an immeasurable amount time and our manners were long gone. I expect you experienced something similar.

"I asked him a question. I don't know exactly what I asked, it was such a long time ago now. But I did say something and when no reply came, I figured he would return soon.

"He never did. So I waited under a tree and met several creatures who wondered why I was waiting. Each time I said for my brother to come back and each time, they shrugged and continued on their way.

"It was about this time that I understood that he was not returning. I left my spot under the tree and made my way through the woods as we intended when we began.

"I came to a river, where I met an interesting person. I needed to go across the river to go down the path but when I peered over it, I saw nothing going that direction. No trail, no path, only a dense patch of trees.

"I asked the woman with a boat if she could take me across and he told me that nothing was that way. Only the way I came, upstream, and downstream.

"I remember her quite well. She was not very tall, shorter than me at the time, in fact. Curious about me, she noticed my arms full of the blue flowers. They were faded by then, but not brown. She asked me what they were for if I recall correctly.

"Silly me had forgotten all about why I had ever gone into the woods in the first place. I even forgot my own brother. How? Well it turns out, that when I told her I wasn't sure, she took me down the river to the village you are now in.

"I was brought forth in front of the ruler of the small community at the time. His name was Gen. He was a nice old fellow and the kind ruler of the farming community. He was the one who told me about the blue flowers and how I could have lost my memory. It was some mushrooms I ate you see. The very same that you have eaten. They were more widespread at the time, however.

"Ignorant of my own purpose, he offered me a place to stay for as long as I wanted to sort myself out. I took him up on the offer.

"What happened between now and then is of little excitement I assure you, save me assuming the leadership under Gen's mentorship. He had grown fond of me and with no children of his own, took me under his wing.

"Often, I wondered why I stayed all these years but when I came to realize I had a life beyond this land, I knew nothing was waiting for me back in what I once called home.

"My memory was slow returning you see, and by time all of it, or at least what I assume is all of it, I had built myself quite a home to live in, among my people.

"I then gained a threefold purpose. Lead a peaceful settlement, remove those awful mushrooms once and for all, and find my brother.

"Two I have done. My brother is still lost and I fear I may never find him, but what is living without some hope? As you see, there are ways out of this land if that is what you wish. I can tell you how if you would like. I know you must be out of place, all of you, and knowing how that feels when it is too late makes me want to help anyway I can, since we may have time yet.

"There is a way to get out. Many ways known and more unknown. I can set a guide for you down the safest route, but I must warn that if I am too late to help you, then you may fit in less than you do here when you return.

"That is why many travelers stay once they feel at ease here. I had no intention of returning. I cannot until I find my brother. I had many adventures in doing so but those are for another time, and I fear we have wasted much of it already.

"So I ask, if you complete a favor for me on your way, would you take a guide with you to find a way out? Or would you like me to set a place for you here?

Chapter 13

The three companions had finished their food and were thinking in silence.

The story Freida had told them was riddled with questions.

The Queen noticed and agreed to give them time to think it over, although she cautioned not too much time.

Once the room had emptied, they began to discuss how to move on.

"I believe she is not speaking all she knows," Oslo said, his wings crossed.

Crow paced back and forth across the table, "I think that as well, but think it over Oslo. None of us can remember very well the time we ate those devilish mushrooms and the fact that our young companion here is not as young as he was."

Neil had been thinking that over himself. It was an odd sensation to have. There were stretches of time, hours, that felt like days between anything of note happening. He himself could not remember why they had come to this place. All he ever knew was Crow. Then meeting Oslo. He feared what Freida warned had come true. He had lost his place in the world.

He had been on his journey too long.

"Why did we come here, Crow?"

She paused and looked at him. "To find a quicker way to get you pumpkins. Have you forgotten already?"

Neil nodded even as he began to recall the events of the last several "days". As Crow retold those events, he was more certain than ever that he was under the same spell that Freida was.

"I think we should follow the guide that Freida offered. I want to go home. Before I forget. Oslo, don't you miss your home? Crow? Your family?"

Both birds became still and thought over his words. He made them feel nostalgic for their homes. It was true. For Oslo, it had been some time since he had gone back to where he was born all those years ago. Owls live far older than we assume, and since they remember near everything, home is rarely forgotten.

For Crow, it was a rather different story. You see, she had been traveling across the countryside on her way to her home already when she came across Neil. Her instinct to move around from her birthplace, much like other birds, had her use her wings to explore.

Yet unlike her kin, she preferred to not stray more than a few days beyond her home, and she wondered what her fellow crows thought of her.

It was to be a surprise that she had come back from her travels, so she decided to not tell a soul of her pending arrival.

This made the choice easier in ensuring young Neil's journey was as safe as possible.

"Heavens, I could hardly remember seeing my home anymore after so long of being on my own. It has been years since I last was there," Oslo said.

The great Owl's story was a tad more complex than that of his counterparts. He was an only owling and once he spread his great feathers, it was time he ventured off on his own, or so he was told.

Owls rarely tell anything they deem untrue, so he took it to heart and when he left his home, he had not returned. Over time he moved further and further away in solitude, meeting various companions along his quest to see the world and what it had to offer.

The two he now had spent some time with were becoming a sort of family in their own right. Not seeing his for so long, it was he thought he never would remember. He was rather starting to enjoy such feelings.

Those feelings left him unsure if he wanted to split up the trio to find the family back where he was born.

This was seen by Crow, who put a wing on his.

Oslo nodded, "You are right my good man. I do believe that we ought to find a way to get you home."

"So it is agreed. We shall accept whatever favor that Freida has given us."

Oslo was still unsure. "Why would she offer us to stay for no price but for us to use her guide, we must complete a favor?"

Crow cawed in laughter, "It is no risk keeping us but certainly it is not easy to venture out for strangers. She doesn't know us like we do."

"Yes, Oslo, I am sure it will be fine. Besides, wouldn't we rather have someone who knows the woods guide us than us getting lost again? We can't use your flight so this may be the best choice," Neil said.

Crow flew around to find the attendee for Freida and told him that they would accept her offer for a guide in exchange for a favor.

She came out shortly after and looked pleased, "Now, let us get you home."

Chapter 14

The trio was introduced to their guide, Ms. Pen. While the two birds were talking the directives with her, Neil was held back with Freida.

"I suppose you should know the favor I ask. Well, it is really quite simple. I need you to take this invitation to a nearby group. It lies on the same path you will be taking."

He took the dull brown document, "May I ask what it is for?"

"Certainly. It is for an upcoming festival we are having later in the season. I also wanted to give you a gift," Freida said as she took a small box from someone nearby.

"These are some of our seeds from the pumpkin crop. We also have some grown ones, but I wouldn't think you could carry all of it."

"Thank you, but how did you know? I barely knew myself."

"Crow told me. She is quite perceptive. I admit, I didn't think it was something that would be asked, but her story made me happy to give anything I can."

With that, the party was off. Ms. Pen was kind enough and made pleasant conversation, giving Oslo someone to make friends with again.

Crow laughed to Neil that he was beginning to not act like an Owl but a hummingbird, more inclined to talk than listen.

The feeling was overall a cheerful one. Neil, Crow, and their Owl friend were happy to have someone who knew their way about to take them to their homes.

The mood around them happened to change as well. Sunlight was creeping through to give a natural glow.

The chirping of sound birds was heard for the first time in their recent memory.

"Ms. Pen," Neil asked, "can you tell us anything about this village we are to take the invitation too?"

She smiled. Now, she was a tall, lounging Falling with a lighter complexion than the rest of the town they were in, giving her a youthful appearance. Owl was talking to the two earlier about how they aged slower than most animals or creatures they knew of. Except turtles and owls, of course.

So although the lighter complexion of the orange could be due to her young age, compared to the rest of her kin, she very well could be older than even Oslo.

"Yes! They are kind people, much like my own. They settled near a river, so they aren't as proficient in farming as we are. They make their living as fishers and hunters.

"They provide a good source of trade for us. We give them crops, they give fish and safe travels on the water."

As they approached a main road, the pathway widened and more travelers were on their way to their destinations.

"I had no idea that anyone lived here like this," Neil whispered to Crow.

She nodded, "Nor did I. Apparently there is an entire world here separate from where you or I live."

"If we hadn't a want to go home, I would love to explore this as much as I could."

Crow noticed that even as he had seemingly gotten older due to the effects of the woods, he was still the boy who was old enough to enjoy exploring but young enough to be more curious than anyone around him.

If Crows could smile, she would have. As you know, it is difficult to smile with a beak. Otherwise, you would appear to be like a crocodile with no teeth.

"I am sure you would. Maybe we can come back," Crow said.

"Oh, I don't know. I may not leave. Have we thought about if I have been here so long that my family doesn't know who I am?"

He was becoming downtrodden and showed no attempt to hide it.

"One thing I have learned, is that family does not forget who you are if they truly love you. Do you they love you, Neil?" Crow asked.

"I believe they do."

"Then they have not forgot you. They simply have waited for you, no matter how long it has been. Perhaps they have been worried, but they have not forgotten you."

"Do you promise?"

"I promise with all my heart. If I didn't, I would not have been going home before I met you."

Both moved along in silence. The Owl was still talking to Ms. Pen.

"I am sorry about keeping you from seeing your own family," Neil said.

"Don't be. I chose to help and don't regret it. Besides, what kind of Crow would I be if I didn't stop and offer help?"

She hugged her wing around his neck and he laughed.

The mood shifted once more to that of happiness and optimism.

A short amount of time later, they arrived to what looked like tall hedges with an arched opening in them. It was reasonable to say they had arrived at the river village.

"This way, this way, hurry along!" Ms. Pen shooed them from behind, although trying not to ruffle any feathers.

Neil did not need any shooing; he went through the archway and what he saw made him open his mouth in awe.

The Falling town they had left was a rather rustic looking place, with simple structures and colors, but done in a tasteful fashion.

This place was that but so much more. The theme of the buildings were various shades of blue and aqua colors. They were taller than the hedges, which was impressive since the hedges were the largest he had ever seen.

Each building was painted in different patterns. Swirls and large fishes, flowers and river birds decorated the schemes. Brilliant lamps were on each corner of them, all shaped liked coiled coral shells.

The colors varied from building to building. There was no light coming from the as of yet but he could imagine what it would look like once night fell.

The entire scene looked like it belonged in a painting or crystal display. Even those who walked by were different. They were paler than those of Freida's followers. A pale blue was all he could think of but he knew it did no justice to their appearance.

Each who walked by smiled just as their neighbors, but it was out of politeness of walking by someone standing in their way.

Crow and Owl were just as speechless. Ms. Pen smiled.

How could two so different things exist here?

Neil noticed that the sun was now out from behind the clouds. The Falling town had been cloudy due to the time of year, but with no wind, nothing removed the clouds. Here, the river weather provided movement to have the clouds be moved to see the sun.

He supposed that they were as pale as their new neighbors. But that would soon change the longer they stayed near the water, which was not too far from them.

"You go along and see the river; it really is a wonder. I must see when the council can see us," Ms. Pen said as she walked off.

The trio made their way to the water's edge.

The whole town seemed to be long lengthwise but not very wide. The water was a brilliant color of blue. Small docks dotted the beachline as boats of various sizes lined them.

From little fishing boats to larger sailboats with boxes stacked on them, it seemed to be busy that time of day. It was hard to imagine it not being busy, considering that they had not seen anything else along the waterways ready for trade.

The dock at Mr. Trinket's farm was nothing compared to this. Neil wondered if the river he had rowed them down was connected to this one they were watching.

Did they know such a thing existed? Were they even in the same woods as the Tom and Mr. Trinket?

One has to understand the complex nature of their journey. They went from a dark, foreboding place to one filled with kind and interesting creatures. Connecting them was a hard task, as the differences in the sky was hard to ignore.

Surly they were in the same woods but not the same place. Venturing in too many directions to keep track had them explore all sorts of things.

The current river's edge had town residents moving this way and that, loading and unloading crates of goods that were unseen.

From what they knew about the town, it was reasonable to say the crates were filled with food from the Falling town residents or materials to help build more beautiful buildings.

Resisting the urge to go and find out, the trio was about to go find their guide when she found them instead.

With her was a short looking fellow dressed in a green suit. His hat was tall and covered with what appeared to be grass that grew from the sides of the river.

It was something Neil had noticed from Freida. The leader of each town seemingly dressed according to where they lived.

This man's expression was painful looking, as if he had too much on his mind to be bothered by a young man, a Crow, and an astute looking Owl looking to correct him on anything he said.

What a trio they had become. All had become used to each other and had become a little family away from family.

"Friends, this is Mayor Corly. He was delighted to receive our invitation from well-traveled folks such as yourselves," Ms. Pen said, introducing him.

"If that is his delighted face, I'd hate to see what being sad looks like," Oslo said, under his breath.

Crow stifled a laugh and slapped him unnoticed with her right wing.

Neil coughed and then reached out his hand in greeting.

Corly looked down and grimaced. He was not a fan of handshakes it appeared.

Neil brought his hand back.

"Terribly sorry but I prefer to not spread where my hands have been to people I do not know."

Oslo snorted as only a large bird could do.

It was now known silently among them that they would not be staying long in this town, no matter how pretty it was.

"I understand, my mother always told me to be careful not to spread germs too," Neil said, forcing a smile.

Corly grimaced again, "Quite."

Ms. Pen saw the tension and, bless her soul, moved the conversation along.

The Mayor was pleased to meet them and was granting them safe passage on a boat he would provide downstream on their journey. Neil was thrilled to see more of the river, Crow was happy to move again, and the Owl could not determine if it were due to a favor to Freida or that Corly didn't like strangers and would do anything to get rid of them.

Crow told Oslo to keep it to himself but as she talked with Ms. Pen and Corly, he and Neil debated the matter.

Before long, they were off just as fast as they had arrived.

Chapter 15

The four travelers were on their way down the river. It was bright and warm, with white colored river birds dashing this way and that, along the sides of their sailboat.

The craft was one that was special to the Mayor himself, something that Oslo thought amusing. Crow was not with them as she thought it good sport to fly with the river birds.

Neil thought that it was good for her ,as it had been sometime since she was able to spread her wings.

There was a sinking feeling, among all the positive ones, that something dreadful could happen soon. It was hard to shake.

"Ms. Pen, I do hate to interrupt, but may I ask where we are headed?"

She was talking to the boat's captain.

"Certainly. There is a road in which you can get onto, taking you back home straightaway. Although, I do hope we avoid the dark."

"Dark?" the great Owl cocked his head.

"Oh yes, the entrance to the road is an old one. But I hear that Neil here must get to a Mr. Dodson's farm for some pumpkins."

Neil dug around his pocket and produced his seeds that Freida gave him, "I have these. They should do."

"Oh no! They very well will not be all you take home! Your mother sent for pumpkins and you shall have them!"

"The dark. Ms. Pen you mentioned the dark?" Oslo seemed impatient.

"Yes, yes. To get to the road, the river winds through a rather dark place full of some unsavory characters. That is why it was generous of Mayor Corly to lend us his official vessel to get safe passage."

She stopped speaking and looked at the two standing a few feet away from her. She could see their confusion.

"There is a lot more in these parts than what you have seen. Some of it good, like the kind Freida and her people, and others not so much. Like the unkind man you met early in your journey. For ages that's how it has been. And for ages to come I imagine. But since you are on a time schedule now, I shall not tire you with storytelling. Besides, we are just about at our stop."

She pointed just ahead of the bend in the river. A stone dock was all that stood in the water. On the shoreline, was a square, stone building.

The boat slowly arrived at the dock and they disembarked.

They said goodbye to their captain and turned their attention to the road that started near the building.

It would have been dark, as the sun had set by this stage, but lanterns on slender trees dotted the sides, giving enough light to travel without getting lost.

"This way. We should get a move on and we will get to the gate soon enough," Ms. Pen said as she started down the road.

The trio followed close by. The air had cooled considerably after being in the sun for the previous whole day. It was a sensation none of them enjoyed and they felt rather empty after seeing the sun moving away once more.

But the overall hope was that they were all almost home.

"The way we are traveling should allow us to remain unnoticed or unmet by anything," Ms. Pen said quietly.

Neil was confused on why she had lowered her voice despite them being all alone on the road. Or so she said. Perhaps it was more of a reassurance than anything, as to not frighten them.

Crow and Oslo glanced at one another. Then, at Neil. They thought the same thing that he did. And as he did, they mentioned nothing of it out loud. He considered that it could be for her own sanity as much as theirs.

So as long as they got home safely, that was all that mattered to them.

They ventured onward to a new road. This one was not as smooth as the ones in the villages. It was slightly overgrown with moss on both sides of the hardened, clay foundation.

There were spots along it that were soggy from dew and rainfall that must have passed through not long before they arrived. The entirety of the atmosphere reminded Neil of the woods around Mr. Trinket's lantern farm, but somehow darker, if that were possible.

In the distance behind the thick trees, there were sounds of birds he had never heard before. That was a good sign. Life here meant that it was not so horrible as it could be. Not being able to see them, however, was a downside he wished could change.

After several hours of walking, and in this place, it might have well been days gone by.

They came to what was a stone wall, resting on either side of the tree line.

It was here that Ms. Pen stopped in her tracks and folded her arms.

"I am afraid I must relieve my guide duties here and leave you to your own. I only am allowed to travel as far. This is what you could call the border of my land."

The trio looked at each other.

Crow hopped to Neil's shoulder to get to a higher vantage point, "We thank you for getting us this far, but what should we expect from this gate?"

"Nothing you have not already met before. I imagine you will come across nothing. Just a few miles beyond this is Mr. Dodson's farm then from there, you can go home."

"A few miles? That doesn't sound too bad," Oslo said, "Perhaps we will meet a few new friends along the way."

Neil smiled. The change in their Owl friend was as much as anything he and Crow had gone through.

"What will happen to me?" he asked, curious about his aging process.

"I don't know. Freida never told me. I imagine you should go back to what you were before you came here."

"Cheer up Neil," Oslo said, putting a big wing around him, "I am sure you will still remember all the good times we have had. And the bad, but that only makes you appreciate it all even more."

The reassurance made him feel better, but what he wanted to know but refused to ask, in fear of the answer, was if he would keep all the memories of his adventures. He quite enjoyed his time with Crow and the Owl.

It would be a shame to forget such things. They could be stories he would tell his children. Besides, what was to keep him from going back? Going home was on his mind, but if home was different, nothing kept him from returning the place he had discovered and finding out all of its secrets. Surly there was plenty to keep him occupied.

He could ask Freida for work. A place to live. He could learn to farm. Or fish and go on adventures down the wild rivers. He could find the Tom Cat and see if he truly were mad.

If indeed his story were to end once he left, he would think it a grand thing to have experienced, even if he still didn't do as much as he could have.

Once he left he found it hard to believe that he would simply forget the whole ordeal.

He shook his head as he heard voices asking him something.

It was Crow. "Should we continue on? Or do we need a rest?"

"No need. I shall be OK."

They marched onward.

It was a few minutes before they crossed the gate's border and found themselves on a path nestled between rolling, flowered hills.

Th dramatic shift from the darkened woods to a bright, open field surprised all of them.

"I hope we don't have to walk miles and miles. I am too tired to fly. I don't think I handle any more weeks of walking."

The great Owl lugged along in between the other two.

"I agree, but then again I am able to fly when you cannot. But cheer up," said Crow, "we are nearly done as Ms. Pen explained to us."

He grumbled, "I still liked the boat because we didn't have to do anything."

Neil laughed, "Oh come now, Oslo, it's not natural for a great creature such as yourself to be cooped up on a boat, letting someone else be the magnificent one."

This made the Owl straighten a little and puff his chest out.

"You are absolutely right; I think I have become too soft. Let us carry on, I shall go see what lies ahead."

With that he flapped his great wings and took off to the sky.

"Good thinking," Crow said, "I feel he has been out of place not being to fly so long. He lost his taste for it. We only needed to do some fine massaging on his ego."

Neil nodded. His mother always told him that in order to help people be their best, they sometimes needed to believe in themselves first.

For their Owl friend, knowing that he could still have people in awe of his talents was that belief. Crow said it was because he and his kin were expected to be magnificent and if they could not be that, then they were of little importance.

Neil was told they were the wisest, which was proven true but he could see the pressure that Oslo could be put under to live up to such expectations.

That being said, he did not return after flying off.

Crow and Neil glanced at the other and hurried ahead.

There was nothing near them except the hills and grass.

They began to call out.

"OSLO!"

"Come on friend, where are you?"

Not a single sound could be heard except unseen birds in the distance and the mooing of livestock.

Where had they gone too now?

They came upon a wide-open pastureland that had a tall metal wire fence. Livestock of various kinds roamed the grass, eating or sunning to their hearts content.

There was a sign just to the right of the fence gate.

It read: "Dodson Pastures."

They had made it to their destination. Time to find their friend.

Chapter 16

A large, red barn was the center piece of the area. A tan house stood to the right of it, a few dozen yards away.

Behind the large barn was more grass, however, this was greener than what they had seen before they arrived.

The pair stood just inside the gate, unsure of how to continue.

A voice called out, "Hello there! Can I help?"

It was that of a man's voice.

He came up them smiling. He was tall with curls of red hair sticking out from under his corn straw hat. He was wearing a green square patterned shirt, with blue jean overalls.

A piece of straw was poking out from the right side of his mouth.

Crow was the first to respond. "Actually, our visit is two-fold. We were wondering first if you happened to see our Owl friend fly through here?"

He nodded, "Yes. He came in, then wanted to check out my fields out back before he went back to you. Poor fella actually laid on some hay and fell asleep. I thought it a shame to wake him. I figured you would be close behind soon enough."

"I assume you are Mr. Dodson?" Neil asked.

"That I am, young man. Pleasure to meet you...?" Mr. Dodson said, raising one eyebrow in question.

"Neil," he stuck out his hand in greeting.

They shook hands. "Well, since you are here, let us go wake you friend. Where are all of you from?"

He led them to the barn.

"Originally from all over. We have however, had quite a time going through the woods just behind the hills just out past your land," Crow said, flying and landing on Neil's shoulder.

"The woods you say. Interesting. Haven't met many folks who come out of there."

Neil spoke up, "They heard of you. We came here originally to find some pumpkins from you. We got lost but friendly people led us on the right way. Especially a Queen Freida. She was the one who got us help."

Crow was waking Oslo at this time, who was dazed and utterly grouchy for being woken up.

Mr. Dodson turned to Neil. "Freida?

He looked as if he had seen a spirit, "She wouldn't happen to have smooth brown hair would she?"

She did.

"And have an affection for the color yellow?"

She did.

"Yes, as I thought, that would be my sister. I don't suppose she mentioned me?"

The Owl spoke for the first time, "Quite the contrary good sir. She has not the faintest idea you live here, let alone alive."

Mr. Dodson brushed it off. "I don't expect she would. She is forgetful you know. Of the world she left behind."

"She forget her old life so she forgot you?" Neil was having some understanding what all this meant.

"Indeed. Sadly for me, I have sent many a message back but for some reason, she can't grasp that I am stuck here as she is there. However, mine is by choice. I would go in there myself, but the fear of missing my memory is keeping be back.'"

"What do you mean that you are stuck here?" Crow asked.

"I wandered my way here long ago, longer than how I look now. Therefore, I am not certain what would happen if I left my farm and the surrounding land. So, I am stuck.

"Freida is stuck in the same predicament I imagine. Although she seems to have momentary lapses in her memory, whereas I, do not."

Neil had developed a headache listening to the entire ordeal. Who had a memory versus who did not, who was stuck versus who was not. All he had begun to want was to go home.

"At any rate, let us get you a souvenir to take home with you!" Mr. Dodson said as he had led them to a nearby field full of different squashes and pumpkins.

They were magnificent. Some were large and rippled; others were small and smooth. There were medium sized ones that had lopsided stems, giving them a comical appearance.

All were astonishing in color. There were none out of place in sight. In its entirety, the view was nothing they had ever seen. The change of scenery was shocking for the trio who had been in the ever shifting light and dark of the woods.

"Go on, take your pick. However many you want."

"I could not possibly take all I wanted. There are so many!" Neil said.

"Then I am sure glad that you were given those special seeds by my sister," Mr. Dodson said, "but let me give you a small wagon to take home to your mother."

The three got to work selecting their choices. Crow chose the medium sized pumpkins, most with altered looking stems. They varied in the shades of orange but all were a reasonable size.

The Owl got to select the largest of the special squash. He only could choose one for they feared they would not fit more than that going home. So he had taken to be very quiet and alone in his thoughts when picking.

Neil spent his time with the smaller selections. All were in more variety than those in the other choices. He had an enjoyable time selecting, trying to find each different than the last.

Once they all had their picks made, they stacked them into a pile and waited while the kind farmer brought them a wagon.

It was made of wood and the wheels metal. Large enough for all their choices, they piled them in, nice and neat.

"I suppose this is goodbye," Neil said.

"Indeed. To get you home, just follow the road you came in on, continue straight until you reach a fork. Turn right. Walk a few minutes then you should be close to where you began."

"Thank you very much Mr. Dodson," Neil said.

"Tell you folks hello for me."

Neil nodded.

"And you two," he looked down to the two birds, "Be sure to take this young man home safe and sound and then onward to your new journeys yourselves. If you ever need something, any of you, be sure to holler at me."

They all said their goodbyes, reached the road, turned right, then made their way down with Mr. Dodson waving at them.

"Oh, and if you see my sister again," he shouted, "tell her I'm thinking of her!"

Chapter 17

The trio had found themselves at the fork in the road. Neil was to go right. Oslo wanted to see what was left but agreed to follow just a bit further.

Neil walked a few steps before he realized that his two friends were not beside him.

"Are you not coming with me?"

Crow fluttered to his shoulder. "If you look just there, you are close to your house."

He looked where she was pointing her wing and saw she was right. They had traveled further than he knew. They were back well before where he had first met Crow.

"So I will you leave here and watch you go in. It should be special, seeing your mother again."

Neil began to tear up. This was the last time he would see them for a while. That much he knew for certain.

He hugged them both.

"Safe travels Neil," said the great Owl, "I hope you find things never found before. And when we meet again you can tell all of your grand stories."

Crow was next, "Goodluck Neil. I was happy to be able to have this adventure and I simply cannot think of any others, other than you two, I would want to spend this time with."

All had tears in their eyes and Neil nestled into their wings before standing upright, grabbing the handle to the wagon, and walking bravely towards his home.

As he approached the doorstep, his mother opened the door and smiled, "Back so soon? How was the trip to Mr. Dodson's? Bring anything good back?"

Neil ran up and hugged her. Pulling away he glanced back to the fence line. He saw the great brown owl fly away deep into the sky and saw nothing but a Crow, perched on a piece of wood.

He swore that he could see it waving and could not wait to head back to the tree where they met, go over the bridge and see all his friends again.

"Of course! I followed all your advice and made awesome discoveries!"

"Did you now? Tell me all about it while we make pie."

When life hands one an opportunity, sometimes it is best to leap into the unknown, because maybe, just maybe, you can have a great adventure and make memories you will never forget. So when you see a Crow, or an Owl, or a mischievous Tom Cat, keep a keen eye on where they are going, you never know where they will lead you.

End